Siesta

BY **Ginger Foglesong Guy**

PICTURES BY **René King Moreno**

SCHOLASTIC INC.
New York Toronto London Auckland Sydney
Mexico City New Delhi Hong Kong Buenos Aires

Ven, osito.
Come, little bear.

¿Qué necesitamos? What do we need?

Mi mochila azul. My blue backpack.

¿Algo más?
Anything else?

Mi chaqueta roja.
My red jacket.

¿Algo más? Anything else?

Mi flauta verde. **My** green **flute.**

¿Algo más? Anything else?

Mi libro amarillo. My yellow book.

¿Algo más? Anything else?

Mi linterna negra. My black flashlight.

¿Algo más?
Anything else?

Mi reloj blanco. My white clock.

¿Algo más?
Anything else?

¡Sí! Algo azul, rojo, verde, amarillo, negro, y blanco.
Yes! Something blue, red, green, yellow, black, and white.

Mi manta.

My blanket.

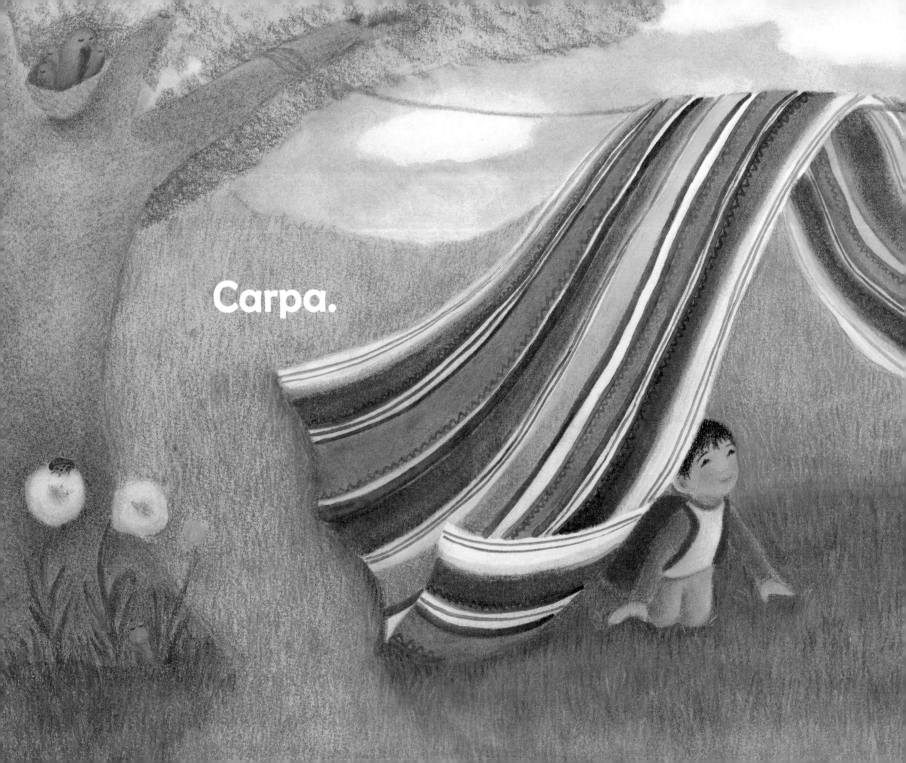

Carpa.

Tent.

Canción.

Song.

Descansa, descansa, osito, mi amigo.
Descansa, descansa, to sleep, a dormir.

Lie still and rest, little bear, my friend.
Lie still and rest, to sleep, a dormir.

Nap.

Siesta.

For Bob Smalldridge, my second father—G. F. G.

For Olivia—R. K. M.

Pastels, watercolors, and pencils were used to prepare the full-color art. The text type is BerlinSans-Roma.

Text copyright © 2005 by Ginger Foglesong Guy.
Illustrations copyright © 2005 by René King Moreno.

All rights reserved. Published by Scholastic Inc., 557 Broadway, New York, NY 10012, by arrangement with HarperCollins Publishers.
Printed in the U.S.A.

ISBN-13: 978-0-545-03577-4
ISBN-10: 0-545-03577-5

4 5 6 7 8 9 10   40   16 15 14 13 12 11 10 09 08